SCARY TALES RETOLD™

GOLDILOCKS AND THE THREE GHOSTS

by Wiley Blevins • illustrated by Steve Cox

RED
CHAIR
• PRESS •

Please visit our website at **www.redchairpress.com** for more high-quality products for young readers.

About the Author

Wiley Blevins has taught elementary school in both the United States and South America. He has also written over 70 books for children and 15 for teachers, as well as created reading programs for schools in the U.S. and Asia with Scholastic, Macmillan/McGraw-Hill, Houghton-Mifflin Harcourt, and other publishers. Wiley currently lives and writes in New York City.

About the Artist

Steve Cox lives in London, England. He first designed toys and packaging for other people's characters. But he decided to create his own characters and turned full time to illustrating. When he is not drawing books he plays lead guitar in a rock band.

Publisher's Cataloging-In-Publication Data

Blevins, Wiley.
 Goldilocks and the three ghosts / by Wiley Blevins ; illustrated by Steve Cox.

 pages : illustrations ; cm. -- (Scary tales retold)

 Summary: "Goldilocks may have escaped the wrath of the 3 bears, but her luck runs out when this busy-body stumbles into a haunted house. Young readers will enjoy this grim retelling of the well-known tale."--Provided by publisher.
 Issued also as an ebook.
 ISBN: 978-1-63440-093-0 (library hardcover)
 ISBN: 978-1-63440-094-7 (paperback)

 1. Girls--Juvenile fiction. 2. Ghosts--Juvenile fiction. 3. Haunted houses--Juvenile fiction. 4. Girls--Fiction. 5. Ghosts--Fiction. 6. Haunted houses--Fiction. 7. Fairy tales. 8. Horror tales. I. Cox, Steve, 1961- II. Title. III. Title: Based on (work) Goldilocks and the three bears.

PZ7.B618652 Go 2016
[E]   2015940012

Scary Tales Retold first published by:
Red Chair Press LLC   PO Box 333   South Egremont, MA 01258-0333

Printed in the United States of America
Distributed in the U.S. by Lerner Publisher Services. www.lernerbooks.com

0516 1 CBGF16

Once upon a time, there lived a nosy
little girl. Her hair was golden yellow.
So everyone called her Goldilocks.
Even though her real name was Pam.

One day, Goldilocks walked into the forest.
She came to a large, run-down house.
"Don't go in," whispered the wind.
But Goldilocks was too nosy to listen.
She marched to the front door. Pushed
it open. And stomped inside.

A light flickered in the large living room.
Everything was covered in white cloth and
dust. Spider webs clung to each corner.
It looked like no one lived in this house.
No living person, that is.

But you see dear reader, the house was filled with spiders and dancing skeletons. And in the attic lived a family of ghosts.

Goldilocks looked around. "All this is mine now," she said. "All mine!"

If only Goldilocks had known that ghosts don't like it when you take their things. If only Goldilocks had cared.

So Goldilocks began looking at all her new things. She looked in cabinets. Under chairs. Behind couches. And on every table. She grabbed what she wanted to keep. And tossed the rest.

Dancing skeletons clicked and clacked but Goldilocks was too busy to hear. Finally, she plopped in the middle of her big mess. All her searching had made her hungry.

Goldilocks stomped into the kitchen. She found
cupboards as empty as a mailbox on Sunday.
So she looked for a chair to sit on. A place to
feel sorry for herself. Because what good is a
house with no food?

Goldilocks sat in the biggest chair she found. But it was too hard. Then she sat in the middle-sized chair. But it was too soft. Finally, she sat in the small chair. "This is just right," she said. Goldilocks bounced up and down.

SPLAT!

The chair broke into tiny bits. But Goldilocks
only laughed. "I am getting sleepy," she
yawned. "I need a bed, not a chair. I will
find one that is just right."

So Goldilocks climbed the stairs. They creaked loudly with each step. A strange scratching noise followed behind her. But Goldilocks was too tired to turn around.

Goldilocks trudged to a large
bedroom. In it sat three beds.
Each bed was a different size.

Goldilocks plopped on the biggest bed. But it was too hard. Then she plopped on the middle-sized bed. But it was too soft. Finally, she plopped on the small bed. "This is just right," she said. And Goldilocks fell fast asleep.

While Goldilocks was snoring, the clock struck midnight. And you know dear reader, no good little girl should be away from her home at midnight. But Goldilocks was too busy dreaming to care.

However, someone else in the house cared. Up in the attic, the family of ghosts began to stir. And the last thing these ghosts liked was someone in their house after midnight.

"It is time to haunt the cemetery,"
said the papa ghost.

"I hope it's a chilly night,"
said the mama ghost.

"I hope there are no puppies," said the baby ghost. Because that's what baby ghosts fear most.

The three ghosts floated out of the attic, down the stairs, and into the kitchen.

"Someone has been sitting in my chair,"
said the papa ghost.

"Someone has been sitting in my chair,"
said the mama ghost.

"Someone broke my chair," cried the
baby ghost. "I hope it wasn't a puppy."

The papa ghost looked up.
"That someone is now in our bedroom.
Let's scare that someone away."

The three ghosts floated up the stairs,
through the walls, and into the bedroom.
They gathered around Goldilocks.

"Oh, how fun," said the baby ghost.
"My first scare tonight."

"Ready?" asked the papa ghost.
"On three. 1, 2, 3, . . ."

"BOO!" they all shouted

Goldilocks sat up. Her eyes bugged out. Her
hair stood on end. Then she let out a deep
scream . . .

And Goldilocks was no more.

The ghosts had scared her to death.

You see dear reader, that's what happens to nosy, little children out after midnight.

THE END